KV-406-958

Contents

Copyright © MCMLXXXIV by World International Publishing Limited.
All rights reserved throughout the world.
Published in Great Britain by
World International Publishing Limited
P.O. Box 111, Great Ducie Street, Manchester M60 3BL.
Printed in Belgium.
SBN 7235 7051 5.
Reprinted 1985

The Book That Talked

by Florence M. Blackett

Johnny scribbled over everything. His bedroom walls were in such a mess that his daddy had to scrape off the wallpaper with its pictures of cars and ships, and paint the walls plain white so that they could be washed easily. Any comic, paper or book that Johnny looked at would be covered in squiggles and wiggles in just a few minutes.

The books especially were not a bit happy about this as they had suffered greatly from Johnny's scribbling, and only the new one looked clean and tidy . . . but he knew that wouldn't be for long. Aunt Mary usually gave Johnny some money for his birthday, but this year she had bought him this lovely big book with pictures of animals, and stories written in large lettering so that he could read by himself.

The time came which all the books on the bookshelf were waiting for, when Johnny decided to have a look at his new book. He had a quick glance through it first and then, sure enough, he went to his desk and got out his crayons. Opening the book again he was going to start scribbling over one of the pages when to his amazement the book slammed shut, knocking the crayon right out of his hand, onto the floor.

Johnny stood there hardly knowing what had happened.

Suddenly a voice from the new book said, "Now sit down in that chair and open me properly."

Johnny did as he was told, putting the book on his knee and turning the pages gently. He found he could read the stories, and he enjoyed looking at the pictures.

When Johnny came to the last page he felt quite sorry and was going to go back to the beginning again when the book said, "That will do, put me back onto the table and pick up one of your other books."

Johnny did so and settled down to read it, but after the first few pages, just when he was getting interested, there was this dreadful scribbling and he could not see what the pictures were at all.

Sadly, Johnny laid the book on the table, and once again the voice said, "This time, look through all the others."

Johnny knew exactly what all the books were like because he'd done all the scribbling. Nevertheless he looked through them and when he had finished turning over all the pages he knew every book would have to be destroyed as it was impossible to read them.

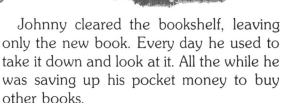

Johnny cleared the bookshelf, leaving only the new book. Every day he used to take it down and look at it. All the while he was saving up his pocket money to buy other books.

The new book never spoke again but Johnny could see how happy it looked when the shelf started to fill up beside it.

Johnny never scribbled again – not in books or comics or on his bedroom wall, so that when his daddy papered his bedroom again, all the ships and cars on the wallpaper stayed bright and shiny with not a pencil mark on them.

Nessie

by Heather Scott

Nessie was a small black and white cat with orange stripes. She was called after the Loch Ness Monster. Nessie kept telling her friends that the Monster was quite friendly . . . but none of them believed her.

"Don't be daft," said her friend, Puds. "The Loch Ness Monster is a dreadful creature. He would just take one look at you and then gobble you up."

"Puds is right," agreed Tabs, the sleek black cat. "If you went anywhere near him your life would be in danger. You are a stupid cat to think he is friendly. Anyway, how can you tell?"

"I'm telling you he IS friendly," argued Nessie. "I only wish I could prove it to you."

"Why don't you bring us a photograph of the Loch Ness Monster with you riding on his back?" laughed Puds. "Then we would all believe how nice he is."

Nessie was getting very annoyed. "You just wait and see if I don't ride on his back," she almost shouted.

"There's only one way to prove I'm right," mused Nessie. "I will go to Loch Ness to see the Monster for myself."

So Nessie started on her long weary journey to see the Loch Ness Monster. She carried her rucksack on her back and her camera case slung over her shoulder. On and on the little cat trudged. She got a few rides from friendly donkeys and at night she slept on top of haycocks. The wild cats she met on her way did not harm her; they even gave her food to eat.

After many days Nessie reached Inverness. She walked quickly through the town and made her way to the shores of Loch Ness. She was so tired when she got there that she lay down and fell fast asleep.

Suddenly she felt a few wet drops on her nose. Nessie opened her eyes sleepily to see the Loch Ness Monster splashing her gently. He looked like a long eel with three big humps on his back. Nessie gave him a friendly grin. The Monster smiled broadly, showing long white teeth.

"The Loch Ness Monster at last," exclaimed Nessie. "I am absolutely delighted to meet you."

"Honoured to make your acquaintance," said the Monster gallantly. "But I don't recall seeing you around these parts before. You must be a stranger. Otherwise you would be afraid of me. I must confess it's dreadfully lonely here. Everyone screams and runs away whenever they see me. The only friend I have is Tommie Turtle."

"Well, you have another friend now," beamed Nessie, "and here comes Tommie Turtle to join us. Would you mind if I climbed on your back?" asked Nessie politely. "Then Tommie could take a photograph of us. It's a special camera and the picture will be ready in seconds."

"Delighted, I'm sure," replied the Loch Ness Monster. "Are you ready, Tommie?"

"All set," replied Tommie. "Both of you give a great big smile."

It was a lovely coloured photograph and Nessie could hardly wait to show it to her friends back home.

"Do please come and see me again soon," said the Loch Ness Monster. Then with a mighty splash he plunged into Loch Ness and disappeared from sight.

Anthony's Useful Present

by Florence M. Blackett

It was Anthony's fourth birthday and he was very excited because the postman had called with lots of birthday cards and presents. He was having some of his friends to tea that afternoon, and his Gran and Grandad were coming to stay and bringing him a birthday present.

Anthony was a bit worried about this present because he had heard his mother talking to Gran on the telephone and she had said, "He'll like that as it will be very *useful*."

Anthony did not like the sound of that one little bit – the word *useful* made him think of dull things like woolly scarves or stockings. What could it be?

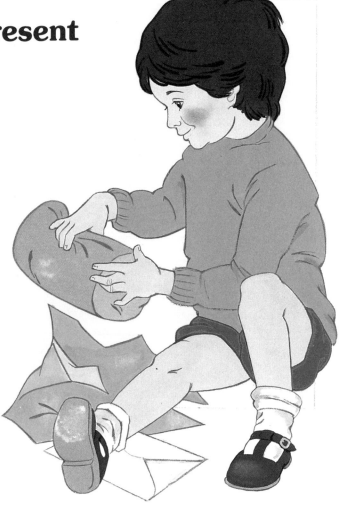

The birthday tea had just finished when the door-bell rang and there stood Anthony's Gran and Grandad. Anthony kissed them both and his Grandad picked him up under one arm while carrying a large funny-shaped parcel under the other, and put them both down in the sitting room.

"Many happy returns, Anthony," said his Grandad, handing him the parcel. Anthony started pulling off the paper, getting more and more excited as he did so. At last there it was – a lovely, large, bright blue wheelbarrow with A.P.B. (standing for Anthony Paul Beckett, Anthony's full name) painted on the side in black paint.

Anthony was delighted and said to his grandparents, "Thank you very much for the lovely present, it will be very *useful*."

Anthony took his wheelbarrow everywhere; he was always using it. One day he went to visit an old lady called Mrs Caine to see if she wanted any shopping. He found her very upset because the coal had not arrived and she had nothing to heat her oven. Anthony thought for a moment and then said, "Why don't we go into the wood and collect some sticks to burn on the stove?"

Mrs Caine said, "That is a good idea, Anthony, but we'd need such a lot, they would be very difficult to carry."

"But I've got my wheelbarrow," said Anthony. "It's exactly what we need for carrying sticks."

Mrs Caine was so pleased and she said, "If you wait a few minutes I'll soon bake some scones for you to take home for your tea."

Just then the coal-man arrived. "I'm so sorry we're late with your coal, Mrs Caine, but we had trouble with the lorry," he said.

"Oh, that's alright, I managed, with the help of Anthony and his *useful* wheelbarrow," said Mrs Caine with a smile.

So Mrs Caine and Anthony with his wheelbarrow walked slowly up the road to the wood, and Anthony ran about filling the wheelbarrow right to the top with sticks and pieces of wood. Very carefully he pushed it back to Mrs Caine's house, and soon they had a lovely fire going in the stove, heating the oven.

The Basketful of Dreams

by Heather Scott

"Gracious me, I've lost my basketful of dreams," muttered Fairy Gelly. "I will go and ask the Wise Old Owl if he saw it."

But the Wise Old Owl had not seen her basket.

"When did you lose it, Fairy Gelly?" he asked.

"This morning," she replied. "I left it under a hedge and went to pick some bluebells in the wood. When I came back the basket was gone. Of course all the dreams are invisible. It's only when I wave my wand that they become true. My basket is full of Birthday Dreams and Dreams for Happy Occasions, too. Would you be kind enough to fly around and look for my basket?" asked Fairy Gelly politely.

"Certainly," hooted the Wise Old Owl as he flew away.

He searched in the treetops and in the tall chimney stacks but he could not find the basketful of dreams.

"Now where did Fairy Gelly say she put her basket down?" he mused. "Oh, yes, beside the hedge in the lane to the wood. I'll go there and have a look."

The Wise Old Owl flew over the hedge three times. The third time he just spotted the handle of a basket almost covered with leaves. Mr and Mrs Blackbird were flying back with straw and feathers to line the basket. The baby blackbirds lay in the grass.

The owl was exceedingly angry when he saw the basket. He thought the blackbirds had stolen it.

"What's all this about, Mr Blackbird?" asked the Wise Old Owl sternly. "That's Fairy Gelly's basketful of dreams."

Poor Mr Blackbird was terribly upset. "My goodness, I really never knew the basket belonged to anyone. I found it lying there and nobody seemed to want it. So I thought it was thrown away."

"You didn't mean any harm," said the Wise Old Owl kindly. "I can see that now. But the basket is full of dreams and the Fairy Queen is to have her Birthday Dream tomorrow. I will fly away and bring Fairy Gelly to collect her basket."

"Please do," chirped Mrs Blackbird. "Tell her how sorry we are."

Soon Fairy Gelly arrived, with the Wise Old Owl flying overhead.

She was very kind to Mr and Mrs Blackbird and told them not to be the least bit worried about taking her basket.

Then she saw the little blackbirds lying in the grass.

"Dear me, Mrs Blackbird, have you no home?" she asked.

"No, we are homeless now," chirped Mrs Blackbird sadly.

"It strikes me that this could be a Happy Occasion, Fairy Gelly," beamed the Wise Old Owl. "At least it would be, if you waved your wand and gave the blackbirds a lovely warm nest."

"What a splendid idea," smiled Fairy Gelly as she waved her wand.

Then a beautiful nest covered with moss and soft white feathers appeared.

"Our dream house," chorused Mr and Mrs Blackbird in delight. "What a lucky day it was for us when we found the basketful of dreams."

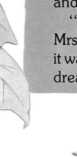

The Froghorn

by Heather Scott

The little blue and white boat lay at anchor in the bay. It belonged to Tim's father. Like all little boys Tim loved the sea, and he was very proud of his father's boat. He loved the shiny black foghorn which stood right in the middle of the deck. The foghorn was just like a motor car horn, except that it had a much louder *honk, honk*.

Tim and his father went out to sea to blow the foghorn to warn the other boats when there was a fog. It was such a pity that they had no name for their boat. Tim's father said that some day they would get just the right name.

On the stone wall beside where the little boat was bobbing up and down, a frog was having great fun. He leapt up in the air, turned somersaults and hopped from one foot to the other.

"Mr Frog," whispered the foghorn. "Something TERRIBLE has happened."

The frog did not hear him at first, so the foghorn whispered a little louder: "Mr Frog, can you hear me?"

The frog heard him this time. He stopped right in the middle of a somersault and asked, "Why are you whispering?" in a surprised voice.

14

"I've lost my loud voice and can only whisper," replied the foghorn. "Tonight I won't be able to warn the other boats that there is going to be a fog."

The frog thought for a moment and then he said, "Let me come on board and I will give a loud *croak, croak* instead of your *honk, honk* and all the boats will hear me." Then he added with a laugh, "I can be a *froghorn.*"

The foghorn did not think it was at all funny.

"A froghorn indeed," he muttered bad-temperedly. "Such nonsense! Whoever heard of a froghorn? Still, I suppose you'd better come along tonight."

Just after tea Tim and his father cast off anchor and set out for sea. The fog was just beginning to rise and soon it would be very thick.

When they were out of the bay, the foghorn whispered to the frog, "Now it's time to give a warning to the other boats. Are you ready?"

"Quite ready," replied the frog, clearing his throat.

Then he gave three load croaks. It was such a funny sound and not at all like the deep *honk, honk* of the foghorn, but it did warn the other boats about the fog.

The frog thought it was great fun. After a little while he gave another loud *croak, croak* – much louder than the first time.

When Tim heard the funny sound he giggled and said, "What a funny noise. It sounded just like a frog croaking. It must have been a froghorn."

"A froghorn?" repeated his father slowly.

Suddenly he remembered how they could never think of a name for their boat.

"That's just the right name for our boat, Tim," he said. "We will call it 'The Froghorn'!" . . . and that is how the little blue and white boat got its name.

The Helpful Sandcrabs

by Sylvia Seymour-Taylor

The Mountain King had a sore throat, and that made him cross with everybody. He sent his two elves to bring his three Advisers.

The first said, "If you can get a woollen scarf and wind it round your neck, your throat will be better."

"Where will I get a woollen scarf?" asked the Mountain King.

"Please, Sire," called out Tip-Toes, one of the elves, "I know an old woman in the valley who knits."

"Order her to knit a long scarf for me quickly," said the cross King.

So Tip-Toes hurried away to the old woman. A few days later he came back carrying a scarf, brightly striped in red and blue.

Eagerly the King wound it round and round his neck. Then he started walking and tripped up on the scarf, and that made him crosser.

"Sire," said his second Adviser, bowing, "may I humbly suggest some liquid honey for helping your sore throat?"

"Red Cap," said the Mountain King, turning to his second elf, "go to the bees and tell them I want their best honey — as fast as you can."

"If you can find a sandcrab, then your throat will get better," were the surprising words from his third Adviser. "And meanwhile I suggest you speak softly."

The astonished King considered this advice, and beckoned his two elves. Speaking softly he told them to find a sandcrab and to bring it to him.

"Not so, my Lord," interrupted the quiet Adviser. "You may recall that I stated that YOU yourself must find a sandcrab if you want to be cured."

"Oh, poor me!" sighed the King.

A cold wind whipped round the mountain as the elves prepared for the journey, loading up a cart with food and wine, and more honey. They all set off next day, the Mountain King's striped scarf wound THREE times round his neck because he didn't wish to trip over it.

Off went Red Cap, and it was not long before he was back holding a large lily. Inside the flower was lots of liquid honey.

The King drank this. It helped a little, but his long white beard became very, very sticky, and his fingers too. This made him even angrier.

"Where is my third Adviser?" he demanded.

"I am here, Sire, at your service," came a quiet voice.

"Cure my sore throat immediately," shouted the Mountain King. "Oh! it is most awfully sore."

Now, as sandcrabs are usually found on the sands of white beaches which are warmed by the sun, the King found it was getting warmer and sunnier as they journeyed along. He even took his red and blue scarf off, as he was becoming too hot.

"Red Cap," whispered Tip-Toes, "we have come a long way. How much further must we go?"

Red Cap, who was tired too, asked the quiet Adviser, who smiled. "In another few days we will see the sea; then our King can look for a sandcrab."

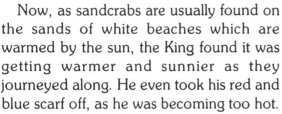

Eventually when they got near the sea, the Mountain King was so hot that he was glad to sit down under some shade. As he was resting on those lovely white sands, he saw first one and then another sandcrab. They were popping up from little holes, running with all their legs and then popping down other little holes. They were so quick that he couldn't catch one. Not even one!

"If I can't catch one I shall never get better," moaned the King.

"But you ARE better, Sire," stated the third wise Adviser. "It does not matter if you catch a sandcrab or not; since you left your chilly mountain home and travelled to this warm, sunny place your sore throat has been cured."

He was right. And the delighted King decided to become King of the Sands instead, and the sandcrabs played with him in a friendly way.

The Bell That Didn't Want To Ring

by Florence M. Blackett

The bells were very excited because they were going to ring for a wedding. All, that is, except Dumpy, the fifth bell. He was in a bad mood because he was tired of being a church bell sitting high up in the bell tower. However, everyone else in the village was very happy because they were all invited to the wedding. The baker was making the wedding-cake, the dressmaker was sewing the bride's and bridesmaids' dresses, and all the men and women were cleaning and getting everything in order for the great day.

One evening the bell-ringers assembled in the tower of the church to practise the bell-ringing.

Ding, dong, ding, dong started to peal the bells joyfully, when suddenly, instead of *ding* from Dumpy, the fifth church bell, there was a horrible clanking sound.

The bell-ringers tried again and again, but the same thing kept happening, so there was only one thing to do, and that was to get the bell to the village blacksmith's forge as quickly as possible to see if he could fix it.

A big lorry was brought and Dumpy hurriedly driven off. When they arrived at the forge Dumpy was lifted down and put on a bench.

After sitting quietly for a while waiting for the blacksmith, Dumpy looked round and was surprised to see a smaller bell with a wooden handle sticking out of its top, looking at him from the other end of the bench.

"Hello," said the smaller bell, "I'm the school bell and my handle is loose, so I'm waiting to be mended."

Dumpy looked quite impressed. "Why, I listen to you every day, ringing to tell the children when to come to school, when it's time to go home, and when it's playtime – I think you are much more useful than I am."

"That's funny," replied the school bell, "I think just the same about you. I listen to you every Sunday and at other important times and wish I was up there in the bell tower ringing loudly. Why, this wedding on Saturday wouldn't be the same without you."

"I hadn't looked at it that way," said Dumpy thoughtfully. "If I tell you something, will you promise never to tell anyone else?"

The school bell looked puzzled but promised. So the church bell went on. "There is absolutely nothing wrong with me at all. The funny sound I was making was because I didn't want to ring properly. I was so fed up with having to ring when my rope was pulled that I decided I wasn't very important anyway and they could do without me."

"Why, that is impossible," said the school bell. "Every bell is needed to make the sound right."

"I realise that now, and I should not have done such a stupid thing. I hope they put me back soon so that I can show everyone how well I *can* ring."

"Here's the blacksmith now," said the school bell excitedly. "As soon as he finds there's nothing wrong with you they'll have you put back in no time."

"Yes, I suppose so, but I must say that the one good thing that has happened is meeting you. Just fancy, you used to ring your bell at school for the two young people when they were children, and now I'm going to ring at the church on Saturday for their wedding. So you see, we're both just as useful as the other," remarked Dumpy.

"That's exactly right," smiled the school bell, "and I don't suppose we'll meet again. But we'll be able to hear each other."

The blacksmith carefully examined Dumpy and, of course, found nothing wrong with him. So he wiped him over and very quickly Dumpy was on the lorry and back in the church tower.

The wedding was a great success and the big church bells rang beautifully – especially Dumpy, the fifth bell – while another smaller bell sat in the schoolroom with his handle fixed, smiling happily.

21

Why Belinda Got Lost

by Florence M. Blackett

Belinda was a fairy who was always knocking into things. She had a large lump on her forehead which she got because she bumped into the large old oak tree in the wood – and sore patches on both of her knees because she kept falling over anything and everything that happened to be in her way.

"Good gracious," her friends would say, "why don't you look where you're going?"

That was the trouble . . . Belinda couldn't see where she was going, but she didn't tell anyone because she didn't want to wear her spectacles.

Belinda was a very pretty fairy and she thought that if she wore her spectacles she would not look so nice. This was very silly of her, because with all the bruises and cuts she was getting, her face was quite black and blue and not pretty at all.

Things went from bad to worse. Her teacher moved her to the front row of the class because she thought Belinda was not taking any interest in her lessons. But her teacher did not know that Belinda could not see what was written on the blackboard.

One morning when Belinda sat down to her breakfast, her mother said, "There is a letter for you." Feeling very excited and wondering who could have written to her, Belinda opened the envelope and written on a card were the words:

WILL YOU PLEASE COME
TO MY PARTY ON
SATURDAY AT 4 O'CLOCK?
CHRISTABEL

On Saturday, Belinda put on her very best dress and flew off to Christabel's. Singing to herself as she went through the wood, and happily swinging the present she'd brought for Christabel, Belinda went past the house belonging to Squirrel Nutkins and then the patch of grass where Robert Rabbit lived. Then she thought she turned at the patch of bramble bushes . . . but then she wasn't sure they *were* bramble bushes as she couldn't see clearly. Anyway she carried on, hoping she was going the right way, but all the trees and bushes looked exactly the same to her, and she had to admit to herself that she was lost.

Sitting down on a branch of a tree she realised that she had landed on Ollie Owl's home, and there he was, looking down at her.

"I'm lost," Belinda cried. "I was going to Christabel's party but I can't go now, it is far too late and the party will be over."

"Yes, I'm afraid so," said Ollie. "It's starting to get dark so I'd better show you the way home."

Coming down to the branch where she was sitting, he said, "I don't understand how you came to lose your way – it's quite easy to find Christabel's house in the daylight."

Belinda felt very ashamed, but she did tell him that she couldn't see very well because she wasn't wearing her spectacles.

"Why ever not?" enquired Ollie. "If you wore them you'd see how many of us in the wood also wear them. I couldn't manage without mine for reading."

Belinda was very surprised to hear this. When she told Ollie that she thought she would wear them in future, Ollie said, "And I should think so too, you don't want to miss any more parties. Anyway, wearing spectacles makes you look very distinguished."

Now Belinda wasn't quite sure what 'distinguished' meant, but it sounded quite nice, and as she flew home close behind Ollie she was pleased that she'd met such a wise old bird.

Belinda's mother was very surprised to see her home so soon and still carrying Christabel's present. But she promised that they would both call round at Christabel's house the next day with it and explain why Belinda hadn't turned up at the party.

Belinda wears her spectacles all the time now and, as Ollie told her she would, she looks very distinguished . . . and happy!

The Story of Horatio

If you ever go to Trafalgar Square in London, and look up to where Nelson's Column stands so high, you'll see lots and lots of pigeons. And among all the grey, brown and creamy pigeons, you might spot a pure white one, perched very proudly on top of Nelson's statue. This pigeon is called Horatio.

Horatio never wanted to be called Horatio. All his friends had names beginning with 'P' and he felt left out and strange because his name started with 'H' and was so old-fashioned. He used to crouch miserably on window ledges, high above the streets of London, wishing his parents had called him Paul, or Patrick, or Percival, or *anything* as long as it began with 'P'. But there he was, stuck with a silly name like Horatio. It was enough to make you cry!

"Why don't you come down to Trafalgar Square?" his friends would ask him. "People buy corn for us and throw it in the air so that we can catch it when it falls. There's plenty of good food there. Why don't you come with us?"

Horatio turned his back and stared at his reflection in the dirty glass of the window. "No," he said stiffly. "I should only be laughed at."

His friends shrugged their shoulders and flew off, back to Trafalgar Square, leaving Horatio staring at himself in the glass. How miserable he was! How ashamed of having a stupid name like Horatio! It was such a stupid name that he was sure people would *know* his name was Horatio as soon as they looked at him, as if in some strange way it was written all over his feathers. So he hunched his shoulders, and stared very grumpily at himself.

"Hello, mate," said a cheery voice from beside him.

He turned his head slightly and saw one of the local sparrows that all the pigeons tended to look down on because they were so cheeky, and because there were so many of them. He looked the other way with his beak in the air and did not reply.

The sparrow fluttered his wings and looked about him. "Nice place you've got here," he remarked. "You don't find many of you pigeons hiding away up here. Usually down in Trafalgar Square and places like that, where all the people spend a fortune on corn for you. What's the matter? Eaten enough?"

Horatio glanced haughtily at him. "Did you want something?" he asked.

The sparrow preened his feathers. "Not really," he said. "It's just that I don't like to see other people sitting about on their own. You looked lonely."

He paused and looked at Horatio. "What's your name anyway?" he asked.

Horatio's beak shot up into the air again. "Why do you want to know?"

"Only being friendly, mate," said the sparrow unconcernedly. "Only being friendly. My name's Albert."

Horatio turned to stare at him. "*Albert?*"

The sparrow met his stare levelly. "Yup! Albert, after that prince who married Queen Victoria. I was born on his Memorial, you know. My mum liked royalty and such."

Horatio smiled wistfully. "I wish I was named after someone. As it is, I'm just Horatio."

"And what's wrong with that?" demanded the sparrow. "If you were called Henry or something, you'd be proud to be named after all those kings, wouldn't you? Well, what's wrong with being named after Nelson?"

Once again, Horatio gaped at him. "*Nelson?* You mean *Nelson* was called *Horatio?*"

The Sparrow nodded. "Of course he was! Everyone know's that. I can't imagine why you didn't know it. Aren't you proud now?"

Horatio nodded. "Oh yes! I wonder why nobody ever told me before. I think I'll go down to Trafalgar Square this minute and tell everyone."

"You do that!" said the sparrow. "You do that, mate! They'll be really impressed, you wait and see."

And they were! They were *very* impressed, and all fluttered up to see the statue on top of the column which was Horatio's namesake. Horatio flew up to sit on Nelson's cocked hat where he was highest, and he sometimes sits there to this day, looking down on all the people passing by, and feeling very proud that he was named after such a great hero.

The Fallen Star

by Sylvia Seymour-Taylor

Early one morning, just when the stars were going to bed, a sleepy one rolled over and fell out of the sky. She fell and fell all the way down to Earth and went *splosh* into a river. One or two of her friends gave a tired twinkle at her to try and guide her back, but soon they fell asleep, having been twinkling in the sky all night long.

So the poor little star lay in the water with no twinkle left in her, and wondered how to get back into the sky.

Some fish swam by, curious, considering how to help. Two silver trout called their friends for a meeting.

"We'll all push her up to the surface," the leader decided. "Gather round in a circle, close together. Now, one, two, three, go!"

The fish gasped as they came out of the water, and with a final push got the star onto the bank. "Oh, thank you!" said the star gratefully.

By now it was noon; the star still had a long way to go.

A flock of starlings flew past, then circled in formation and flew back again, offering to help.

"We'll bring a towel from a clothes-line, and take you up in that," said the birds.

It was a good idea: the little star was taken as far as the highest tree. She thanked them, waved goodbye and sighed.

By now it was afternoon and the star was not nearly there.

How was she going to get back into the sky in time to help light up the world by evening? One star appeared, looking for her friend.

Soon after this a boy walked along under that tall tree, carrying his air-pistol. He happened to look up; the star looked down.

"Please can you help me to get back into the sky?"

"Wait until I climb up. I will shoot you there with my air-pistol." He managed to climb up into the highest branches, but . . . he couldn't get the star into his air-pistol. He fired a shot of annoyance in the direction of the star in the sky, and went home for his supper.

It was starting to get dark by now, and a

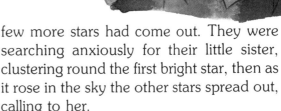

few more stars had come out. They were searching anxiously for their little sister, clustering round the first bright star, then as it rose in the sky the other stars spread out, calling to her.

"Come on, it's evening now. Can't you climb up?"

"How?" she cried pitifully.

Just then she saw a silver thread leading upwards and out of sight, so she climbed up and up the silver thread until she reached her sisters in the heavens. All the stars twinkled in delight.

And a tired little spider, who had once been curled up cosily inside the boy's air-pistol, smiled a big smile, and went to sleep himself now that all was well.

29

The Coffee Morning

by F. M. Blackett

The toys were very unhappy. They were unhappy because there they were in the toy cupboard and nobody had taken them out and played with them for ages. Rag Doll, Teddy Bear, Nodding Dog and Panda, not to mention the boxes of building bricks, jigsaw puzzles and the wooden engine, were all just lying about the shelves and getting sadder and sadder. The most miserable of all was the china pig called Piggy Bank, because not only was he forgotten, he was also empty. No one had put pennies in the slot on his back for a long, long time and he had the same feeling in his tummy as you have when you are very hungry.

"Why don't Timothy and Jane play with us any more?" asked Panda. "Jane used to cuddle me and take me up to bed with her." (Timothy and Jane were the children who owned the toys.)

"My head and tail are very stiff because Timothy hasn't pulled me along the floor for ages, so my head doesn't nod and my tail doesn't wag any more," said Nodding Dog.

"It's no use complaining," sighed Rag Doll. "We can't do anything about it, the children are growing up and have other things to do instead of playing with us."

"Oh, dear," said Teddy Bear, "I hope we don't have to spend the rest of our life shut up in this cupboard." At which awful thought there was a great silence. Piggy Bank didn't say anything at all, he just wanted to be useful again.

One day the toys and Piggy Bank could hear that something was going to happen; they listened carefully and kept hearing the words "coffee morning".

"What is a coffee morning?" whispered one toy to the other.

"Just listen," said Piggy Bank, "and we might hear." He was feeling excited because he'd heard something about making money, and the sound of money always made him happy.

It soon became clear that Timothy and Jane's mother was going to sell cups of coffee to neighbours and friends and the money collected would be given to the children's hospital for Christmas.

When they heard this the toys decided to form a plan.

Meanwhile Jane was making biscuits (crunchy ones made from cornflakes) to be eaten with the coffee, and Timothy was just wandering about, not knowing what to do to help. He was just going past the toy cupboard when suddenly there was a loud bump, and much to his surprise, the cupboard door flew open and Rag Doll, Teddy Bear, Nodding Dog and Panda all landed in a heap on the floor at his feet.

Timothy bent down and started picking them up and shouted to his mother to come and help.

"Oh dear," his mother said when she saw what had happened, "it's about time the toy cupboard was tidied up, these toys have been lying in there for too long." After thinking about it for a moment, she went on, "Well, now, these toys will be just the thing to give to the children in hospital at Christmas, as you and Jane don't play with them any more."

So Timothy started going through the rest of the cupboard. He found the building bricks, jigsaw puzzles, the wooden engine, and Piggy Bank; they could all be given to the hospital . . . except Piggy Bank, he decided.

He rushed to tell his mother about his good idea. "Mummy," he shouted, "can we use Piggy Bank to collect the money from the coffee morning?"

"We certainly can," said his mother. "In fact it will be much better than using a dish or a tin."

Next day the coffee morning was a great success and everyone was very happy. The coffee and biscuits were delicious; Piggy Bank looked very important and useful standing right at the front of the table full up to the brim with money, and Rag Doll and all the other toys were very excited because they were going to be played with again.

Afterwards Timothy said to his mother, "Just fancy, if the toys hadn't fallen out of the cupboard the other night, we might never have thought of giving them to the hospital."

"You are quite right, Timothy," said his mother. "It was really very odd the way it happened."

But we know that the toys planned it that way, don't we?

Spick and Span

by Caroline A. Smith

"I do wish they wouldn't stare so," sniffed Spick. Span just laughed and stuck out his tongue at the little boy who was standing with his nose pressed up against the window.

Suddenly the door behind them opened and Spick and Span felt themselves being lifted through the air. Spick squealed and Span kicked his heels in excitement. What was going to happen?

"Now they look a smart pair of shoes, don't they, James?" a tall, well-dressed lady asked the little boy standing next to her.

Spick was delighted to be thought smart.

He was proud of his shiny, brown leather coat and his fine brown laces. Span shuddered as he heard the lady speak. He wrinkled up his toes and tried to look as untidy as he could. A pair of shoes could hardly have been more different: Spick loved to look smart and Span loved to look scruffy.

James sat down and pulled Spick on to one foot and Span on to the other one.

"They fit perfectly," said James' mother as she pinched Spick and Span's toes.

"Horrible woman!" squeaked Span.

"Ssh!" whispered Spick.

"Yes, we will take this pair," she added to the shop assistant. The girl took Spick and Span, stuffed them with tissue paper, and squeezed them into a box.

"Ooh, it's dark in here!" squeaked Spick.

"And hot," moaned Span. "This paper is making me itch!"

After what seemed like a lot of jerking and bumping Spick and Span could see the lid being lifted off their box. "Look, Dad!" they heard the little boy shout. "My new shoes!"

"They're smashing," they heard a deep voice reply. "Give them to me and I'll put a spot of polish on them for you, then you'll be able to wear them at school tomorrow."

"What's polish?" Span whispered to Spick.

Spick shrugged his shoulders. "I'm not sure, but I've heard that it makes you look smart."

The man leant over their box and lifted Spick out by his heel. Spick winced as the hard brush was rubbed forwards and backwards over his toes, sides and heel. By the time the man had finished he felt quite sore, but when he caught sight of his bright, shiny appearance in the mirror, he felt very proud. Polish might not be nice, but it was worth it if it made him look so smart. Span did not agree. He screwed up his toes and tried to get rid of the horrible sticky polish. He did not want to look smart, and he certainly wasn't going to put up with being battered and bruised by a rotten old brush.

"Well, that's about the best I can do," sighed James' father. "This left one just won't shine as well as the right one."

"Good!" thought Span. "I'll show them."

The next morning Spick and Span were awake early and by eight o'clock they were tied tightly onto James' feet and on their way to their first day at school.

Spick was very aware of how smart he looked. He walked proudly, nodding politely at all the other shoes they passed. "Just look at those ugly Wellington boots!" he said to Span. "How clumsy."

"Much more sensible than us," moaned Span, kicking his toes against the kerb. "At least they don't have to put up with the smell of this horrible polish!"

"Oh, look at those smart high-heels!" Spick cried. "Don't you wish we were like that?"

"No fear," said Span, wrinkling up his toes in distaste. "You wouldn't be able to do anything." And with that he stepped off the kerb and fell right up to his neck in a puddle.

"Oh, no!" Spick began. But it was too late. Span had pulled him in too. Spick shivered as the water flooded in over his sides and squelched around his insides. "Look what you've done now!" he complained. But Span just laughed.

Soon they reached the school playground. Everywhere there were children running and shouting. Spick held back nervously but Span pulled him forward and straight into a game of football. "You take this one!" yelled Span. Spick winced as the ball bounced off his toes. Then he was limping up and down the playground dragged by Span, who was chasing madly after the ball.

Suddenly Span screamed and fell onto his side. "My heel! Someone's torn my heel off!" he sobbed. Very soon Spick and Span found themselves in James' bag and they spent the rest of what should have been their first day at school being carried around in the dark under a pile of books. "Look what a mess you have got us into this time," moaned Spick. "You and your puddles and your football!"

Span just sat in the corner of the bag nursing his heel. It was very painful.

That afternoon Spick and Span were separated for the first time in their lives. On the way home from school James left Span at the shoe mender's shop.

At first Spick enjoyed having their box all to himself, but after a few days he began to miss Span very much. Span could be a nuisance and he did get them into all sorts of scrapes, but he *was* his brother and it was getting rather boring in the box all on his own. So when Spick at last saw the lid of the box lifting and his brother being lowered gently inside he was very pleased. "Where have you been?" he asked. "You look different."

Span looked rather sad for a minute. "I've had a horrible time," he whispered. "I went to this place where they mend broken shoes. My heel was so badly broken that they had to knock it back on with a hammer."

Spick looked horrified. "A hammer?" he repeated.

"Yes," said Span. "And nails. I don't ever want to go back there again. I've decided that I'm going to be good in future. I won't get us into any more trouble. We'll be Spick and Span like we're supposed to be."

"Oh! I'm glad!" said Spick. "And it will be just as much fun, you'll see."

The Magic Rolling Pin

by Moira Stubley

The most beautiful building in the whole of fairyland was the palace of the Fairy Queen. It was set high on a hilltop, with four pointed spires and a clock tower. The Queen's flag flew proudly from the tallest spire and could be seen for miles around.

All the rooms in the palace were magnificent, and the kitchens were particularly grand. Indeed, the Fairy Queen was famous for her banquets. Visiting Kings and Princes loved to dine at the palace. They always tried to discover the secret of how the Fairy Queen served such splendid meals, but they could never find out!

Crispin the cook knew the secret! The meals were always excellent because he had a magic rolling pin. It had been his friend and companion for years. Indeed, Crispin never left the palace without the magic rolling pin tied to his belt. They had worked together for so long in the royal kitchens that they had many happy, funny memories.

Best of all, Crispin liked to remember the days when the rolling pin first came to the palace. At first young Crispin found it hard to remember that whatever food he mentioned while holding the rolling pin would appear at once, by magic. He discovered another thing that he needed to remember—the rolling pin could not spell!

How the two of them laughed about that day, long ago, when Crispin was showing some visitors round the lovely palace grounds. Pausing at the top of the hill, they all looked down at the tiny village in the valley below. "Yes," Crispin told the visitors, "that's where I was born and bred." He pointed to the village with the rolling pin, and at once, a long loaf of crusty bread landed on the floor in front of the startled visitors! (Well, I said the rolling pin could not spell!)

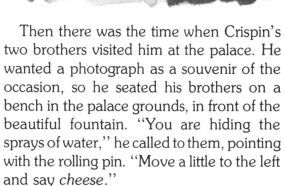

Then there was the time when Crispin's two brothers visited him at the palace. He wanted a photograph as a souvenir of the occasion, so he seated his brothers on a bench in the palace grounds, in front of the beautiful fountain. "You are hiding the sprays of water," he called to them, pointing with the rolling pin. "Move a little to the left and say *cheese*."

Goodness me! In a flash, each brother found a lump of crumbly cheese on his knee! But they never gave away the secret of the magic rolling pin.

All those things happened many years ago, and Crispin loved to remind the rolling pin of those happy days. They would laugh about them as Crispin enjoyed a cup of steaming cocoa in the palace kitchens. But more recently Crispin had become rather anxious. Many years had passed; he was much older. But, worse than that, there were signs that the magic rolling pin was growing old, too. Its memory was simply not as good as it used to be.

Only last week, Crispin had served a delicious dish of roast lamb, potatoes and vegetables. It was one of the Fairy Queen's favourite meals. But the rolling pin had forgotten the mint sauce! And just yesterday, to Crispin's horror, there had been no salt and pepper in the royal hot pot. Whatever was he to do?

There was something else too, and this worried Crispin even more. As it was growing older, his faithful rolling pin was becoming just a tiny bit deaf!

When Crispin had invited some friends to a meal at the palace he had ordered steak and chips. The little party settled down happily at the table, only to find that they were having HAKE and chips. No one had complained, but Crispin was worried. (Suppose it had been CAKE and chips!)

Then there was the morning when a colleague of his came round for coffee. They sat down to find the table set with a huge bowl of TOFFEE. Now that *had* been embarrassing. Crispin knew he would have to speak to the Fairy Queen, otherwise something terrible might happen at a royal banquet. Crispin could not bear the thought of a smart new rolling pin in his kitchens.

One morning Crispin climbed the spiral staircase which led to the great hall, where he was to talk to the Fairy Queen. Crispin dreaded to think what she might say.

The Fairy Queen was most surprised to hear of Crispin's problem. But of one thing she was certain. "Oh, dear me, no!" she proclaimed. "I do not want a new rolling pin in the kitchens. My goodness, we'd be having hamburgers and tinned food every day! No, no, that will not do at all. Crispin," she announced sternly, wagging her finger at him, "you must bring your magic rolling pin to me. Here, tomorrow morning!"

Crispin's knees were shaking even more next morning when, with his faithful rolling pin tied to his belt, he again headed for the great hall.

"Come in, come in," the Fairy Queen called. "Now I shall cover this good old rolling pin in a coat of magic paint. There! He'll be as good as new now, and more magic than ever!"

Crispin breathed a sigh of relief. All would be well. He and his dear old friend could carry on working together again in the palace kitchens.

As they made their way back Crispin and his magic rolling pin sang their favourite song: *Cherry Ripe*. And of course, Crispin ate the juicy cherries which fell by magic into his hands. . . .

The Royal Elephants

by Moira Stubley

The elephants in the Indian palace of Raj Singh were carefully groomed each weekend, so it came as a great surprise one Wednesday morning when the servants arrived with buckets and scrubbing brushes to groom them again.

"Very tiring, all this rubbing and scrubbing," the older elephants mumbled to one another.

"It's rather exciting," whispered the younger ones. "Whatever can be happening?"

The elephants at Raj Singh were the finest in the whole of India. They carried the royal family and their visitors on special ceremonial occasions, so they had to be kept in splendid condition. It was a great honour to be chosen to live at Raj Singh.

One of the youngest elephants, Sansha, had not been chosen. He had been born at Raj Singh. He had been kept on at the palace because his grandfather had been the king's chief elephant many years before. Grandfather was too old now to walk in the royal processions, but he loved to tell Sansha tales of the great days he had known. Sansha grew up hoping and hoping that one day he too might walk in the processions.

On this particular Wednesday Sansha was very excited. He felt that something special was going to happen. By listening carefully to the servants he finally discovered the secret. The young crown prince was coming down to the stables that afternoon to choose an elephant to carry him on royal occasions. Some day, when the prince became king, that elephant would be as important as Sansha's grandfather!

The elephants were lined up for the crown prince, who arrived wearing a splendid golden cloak over his riding tunic. Twice he walked up and down the line, whilst every elephant held its breath in hope. Then Prince Asmir raised his hand and pointed at Sansha.

If elephants could blush, Sansha would have turned bright pink! The prince returned to the palace, and all the servants and elephants gathered round to congratulate Sansha. But Grandfather was the proudest elephant of all. His family would once more carry the royal family of Raj Singh!

For the next two weeks Sansha was groomed and trained, and fitted out with silk and silver trappings. It was all so exciting that at night he would dream of great processions, and each day he practised walking at a dignified pace.

Finally the time came for the first outing. It was a particularly hot day and Prince Asmir wanted to visit the Casmir waterfalls. Sansha was ready, trembling ever so slightly as the young prince mounted his back for the first time.

It was a long, hot journey in the afternoon sun, but Sansha scarcely noticed the heat, he felt so proud. But Prince Asmir was extremely hot. On the return journey he complained to the servants walking beside him that they must fan him more swiftly. He was quite sickly with the heat.

Sansha thought quickly of all the tales his grandfather had told him. Whenever Grandfather had taken the king out on a very hot day, he had always worn his great crown. Though it was heavy, it shielded his head from the intense sun. Yet here was Prince Asmir, high on Sansha's back, with his head completely bare.

The young elephant's trunk stretched out to pluck a huge leaf from a nearby tree. Swinging his trunk backwards, he held the leaf over the prince's head.

At first everyone was startled. Then the servants realised what the clever elephant was doing. "Of course," they cried. "Prince Asmir's head should be covered."

So Sansha dropped the leaf and Prince Asmir put on his round skull cap. The servants waved their fans as fast as they could, and soon the prince felt quite well again.

To Sansha's delight, when Prince Asmir climbed down from his back he stroked the elephant's trunk gratefully. "I see I have made a wise choice," he whispered in Sansha's ear. And from that day the prince was devoted to his elephant.

It was three years later that a strange thing happened. Everyone knew that before long Prince Asmir would become king. He was so fond of Sansha that there seemed no doubt that Sansha would become the king's royal elephant. But the royal elephant must be absolutely obedient at all times.

So everyone was very disturbed when a party of elephants was carrying Prince Asmir and his friends for a ride through the jungle. The prince now rode on Sansha's back seated on a tall, carved throne.

The party was making its way through the trees when Sansha suddenly stopped. He simply refused to move. This was quite unheard of in a royal elephant, and the servants began to slap him sharply.

However, Prince Asmir (remembering that first day, when Sansha had covered his head with a leaf) commanded: "WAIT."

To everyone's amazement he climbed down and whispered in Sansha's ear, "Whatever is the matter, old friend?"

As soon as the prince was off his back Sansha began to move, and as he did so, the royal throne caught in the branches of the trees overhead. The throne was lifted right off Sansha's back and swung dangerously in the air.

"Why, the prince might have been killed," cried the servants.

"You are indeed a royal elephant," the prince said to Sansha.

And he refused to have the throne replaced. Instead, he rode back to Raj Singh seated comfortably on Sansha's broad neck. No royal prince had ever ridden that way before, and Sansha was the proudest elephant in India. What tales he would tell his grandchildren one day!

The Wizard's Search

by George Gilfillan

The wizard yawned, lit his lamp, and drew the curtains across the windows of his cottage. Then he yawned again, sat down in an armchair beside the fire, and closed his eyes.

"I am so tired," he sighed. "Nowadays everyone in the village asks me for a spell. I'm making magic from early morning until late at night. I really must find someone to help me."

He opened his eyes sleepily and watched the logs burning in the fireplace. Suddenly a yellow flame swirled into a ball and two little flames flickered from the top of it. Just for an instant the wizard saw a round head with two sharp ears. There is always a little lost magic drifting round a wizard's cottage....

"Of course!" he cried. "I'll get a cat! A cat can be a great help to a wizard when it comes to making spells."

The next morning he got up early and set off to find a cat.

"It may not be easy," he muttered. "A wizard's cat has got to be black all over. There aren't many like that."

The road he followed went winding through the golden fields of autumn. After some time he saw a farm in the distance.

"That's a likely place," he said. "There are always cats around a farm."

When he reached the farm he saw cats running in all directions. He managed to stop a tabby as it rushed past him.

"Excuse me," he said. "Is there by any chance a black cat on the farm?"

"Oh, you mean Thumper?" panted the tabby. "He's round the back of the barn giving his orders, but I can't stand here talking or I'll be thumped."

And he shot off in the direction of the dairy.

The wizard found a large black cat sitting behind the barn. The cat had pushed its back leg out and was licking its toes. The wizard looked carefully at the cat. He was not sure that he liked it.

"I'm a wizard," he explained. "I'm looking for a cat to help me with my magic."

"I've heard about cats who do that," said the black cat with interest. "How often would we turn people into frogs?"

"Into frogs!" exlaimed the astonished wizard. "Good gracious me! That sort of thing was stopped years ago."

The cat looked disappointed.

The wizard was quite sure that he did not like the cat.

"I'm afraid," he said, "that my spells are not important enough for a cat like you. You would be wasting your time with me."

The wizard went back onto the road and followed it all day. He looked to the right and he looked to the left. He listened for the shuffle of paws in the autumn leaves. He saw cats, but none were black. Towards evening he came to a little town where the houses stood huddled together in the gathering mists.

"In a town," he thought, "there are often poor cats who live in alleys."

It was getting dark and cold. The wizard pulled his cloak tighter around him and went along looking into the passages between the houses. Suddenly he heard a scraping noise. In the shadows he could just see a thin black cat scratching miserably at a bag of rubbish.

43

"Just as well," nodded the wizard. "A cat in a fish shop would find it difficult to keep its mind on the mice."

The street was getting busier. People were going home. They brushed past the wizard as he stood trying to see through the curtains of a tea room window.

"I'll go in," he decided.

A large black cat with a glossy coat was sleeping on a comfortable rug in front of the tea room fire. The wizard had to speak twice to it before it woke up. The cat listened to what he had to say.

"I might think about going with you," it said sleepily. "But you do understand that I have to have cream for breakfast and fish four times a week? And I need my own cushion on a chair of my own that no one else uses. Also, I sleep all morning and most of the afternoon."

"Don't be frightened," he said in a kindly voice. "Tell me something about yourself. Then I'll tell you about my cottage where you could help me with my magic."

The cat sprang into the air. It came down with its back arched, its legs as straight as table legs and its tail standing up like a flagpole.

"Help you!" it hissed, spitting. "You mean work? I've never worked in my life. I won't start now!"

It spun round and vanished into the shadows.

"What a rude cat!" exclaimed the wizard. "I'm glad that it took itself off."

He stood on the pavement, uncertain what to do next. Up and down the little street the shop windows began to light up.

"Ah!" he said. "There will be shop cats who live in shops and keep the mice away."

The wizard went slowly along the street looking in each shop window. The shoe shop had a brown cat, the grocer's shop had a grey cat. The fishmonger did not have a cat.

44

"Perhaps, after all," said the wizard, becoming rather annoyed, "you wouldn't really like to leave the town and live in the country?"

"No," said the cat, "I don't think that I would." It went back to sleep.

The wizard went into the street. He walked along, undecided what to do next. Suddenly he heard a dreadful squeal, and a door ahead of him opened and a black cat flew out onto the pavement. The wizard rushed up to the door. An old lady wearing large spectacles was standing in the doorway with a white cat at her feet.

"Poor Tiddles! Poor Tiddles!" she was saying. "I've done it again."

"Can I help?" asked the wizard.

The old lady turned towards the sound of his voice.

"I can't see very well," she explained. "And I have two cats. I can see my white cat all right, but poor Tiddles is black. I can never see him when it gets dark. I'm always standing on his tail. I do wish I could find him a better home than this one."

"We'll see about that in a moment," said the wizard, and he cast a spell:

> Puss-cat, puss-cat,
> You've had a fright.
> Puss-cat, puss-cat,
> Your tail's all right.

"There now, it won't hurt any more," he said. "As you see, I'm a wizard, and it so happens that I have a comfortable cottage and am looking for a black cat. If Tiddles would like to come and help me with my magic I'd be very pleased to have him."

"I'd love that," said Tiddles.

"Then," said the wizard, "I've found the cat I've been looking for!"

The Lonely Giant

by Moira Stubley

Gyganticus was quite the largest giant in the world. He was also the oldest. All his giant friends and relations had died at least twenty years ago. He was the only giant left, and he was very lonely. So, although he was well over ten feet tall, Gyganticus was afraid. He was such a kind-hearted giant that he was afraid of frightening people. People had forgotten what giants looked like! The last time he had left his house, twenty years ago, he had caused a traffic jam. The drivers were so amazed they turned to look at him and all banged into each other. It was awful. Little children ran away from him, screaming . . . and poor Gyganticus loved little children.

So he was very pleased when a new family moved into the house next to his mansion. Gyganticus' house had huge gardens and very high walls. But if he peeped very carefully over the high walls at the end of the garden he could see the house next door. There were two children, Mandy and Michael, and Gyganticus loved watching them play. His favourite game was the one they played on Saturday mornings, but he always took care that they did not see him peeping. If they ever saw him he could never share in their games again, for they would surely be afraid of him.

Every Saturday they brought out a wonderful black box with knobs, and set it down on the garden table. Then, while Mandy drew pictures and Michael played soldiers, they would listen to the black box. A voice inside the box read out letters from real people, asking for a record to be played for some child's birthday or for a child who was sick in hospital.

Gyganticus thought it was wonderful and so did Mandy and Michael. "I wish someone would write up and ask for a record for us," said Mandy.

Gyganticus puzzled about this. He was such a kind-hearted giant. If he knew where to write he would send up a request for Mandy and Michael. He listened extra hard to the black box and, sure enough, the voice gave out an address to write to.

Back in his house that evening Gyganticus did his best. He lived such a lonely life that he never wrote any letters. But he MUST write to the voice in the black box.

Sir, he began,

I have heard that you play records for little children on Saturday mornings. Two lovely children called Michael and Mandy live in Hideaway House, next door to me. If you read out their names and play a record for them it would make me very happy, because I know they would be excited.

I am,

Yours very sincerely,
Gyganticus

Next Saturday, Gyganticus could hardly wait for the children to turn the knobs on the black box. As the voice and the music went on and on, he kept crossing and uncrossing his big fingers. Then, to his delight, he heard his letter being read out. Mandy and Michael were dancing about with glee as their record was played and Gyganticus began to dance too. He did not hear the record end, but carried on jigging to and fro in pleasure.

"That's Stately Manor over the big wall," Michael cried. "Oh, look, Mandy, a giant, it must be, it must be Gyganticus."

As he heard his name, Gyganticus stopped his jig and blushed a very bright red. Michael and Mandy were running out of the garden. Oh dear! He had frightened them after all. He sat down on a treetrunk and an enormous tear, the size of a marble, trickled down his cheek.

But no! In less than a minute the two children appeared, racing across his lawns.

"Thank you, thank you," they cried. "You are such a kind giant. Please come and play in our garden and listen to our radio."

Gyganticus was so happy he nearly started to cry again. So, with Michael holding one hand and Mandy the other, he left Stately Manor for the first time in twenty years.

The Vain Squirrel

by Moira Stubley

Mr Jackson's garden shed was a perfect playground for squirrels. Some squirrels could sit on the mowing machine and pretend it was a railway engine or a racing car. Other squirrels enjoyed playing house and giving tea parties, with the old plant pots as cups!

But Cecilia Squirrel had no time for silly games like the rest. She had found a brush and comb in one of the drawers. All she would do, day after day, was brush her fine long tail until it was sleek and shiny.

"I have quite the longest tail of all you squirrels," she would announce at least five times each day! It was true. Cecilia was very pretty. But she went on about it so!

"Come and play, Cecilia," the girls would call.

"No, I must curl my hair so that it sits prettily round my ears," Cecilia would answer, ignoring their giggles. Then she would perch on a shelf in front of the large round clock, and use its glass face as a mirror. She purred to herself, "I am as pretty as a picture."

One day, Cecilia did not come to play in the garden shed with the others. They were all enjoying their games when there was a loud "BOOM" from the clock.

"Where is that silly, vain Cecilia?" the clock asked.

The squirrels all stared at him in amazement. "We didn't know you could talk," they said.

"Indeed I can," the clock replied. "And I'd love to tell that Cecilia a thing or two!"

"Oh, Cecilia won't be here today," the girls explained. "There's a party tonight and it will take her ages to decide which ribbons to wear in her hair."

"BOOM!" said the clock again. "Well, I intend to teach her a lesson. You," – he looked straight at a boy squirrel – "come up here on my shelf." So up he hopped. "Now, if you open the hinges carefully you can take off my glass face."

The squirrel did as he was told and hid the glass carefully in a drawer.

"Tomorrow," the clock promised, "Cecilia will learn her lesson!"

Next morning as usual the squirrels gathered in the garden shed.

Cecilia was a little tired after the party. She yawned and stretched herself daintily. Then, sure enough, she hopped up onto the shelf in front of the clock. "I'll arrange my curls differently today," she murmured. "Just for a change."

But, suddenly, the small hand of the clock stretched out and pulled hard at her precious curls. Cecilia let out a shriek and turned round on the shelf.

"Whatever happened?" she called to the others. "My curls, my lovely curls, someone pulled them!"

Now her back was to the clock. So his large hand reached out and gave her tail a great, hard shake.

"What in the world is happening?" Cecilia cried in alarm. "My tail, my tail! I'm sure some of the hair has fallen out!"

Then she noticed that all the other squirrels were laughing. Suddenly the clock, who could not keep quiet a moment longer, also let out a loud boom of laughter.

Cecilia was trembling with fear and anger. "You made a plot," she accused the squirrels. "You're jealous of my hair and you're all quite, quite horrid."

She was in tears now, so the clock stretched out his big hand and patted her gently on the head.

"You silly girl," he said in a kindly voice. "It was all my idea. Your friends are just enjoying the joke. You waste so much time brushing and combing your hair when you could be having fun with the others!"

"But you pulled my hair," Cecilia complained in a small voice.

"And you look much better, my dear, with a few hairs out of place," the clock replied. "Forget your curls and your tail today. Play with the other squirrels."

"But . . ." Cecilia began. Then she saw the clock's little hand reaching out towards her again. Quick as a flash, she jumped down and joined in the games with the others.

Next day, the clock had its glass face on again. Cecilia climbed upon the shelf and tapped on the glass.

"I enjoyed the games yesterday, Mr. Clock," she said. "Thank you for teaching me a lesson."

And the clock was so pleased that he struck twelve, there and then, though it was only eight o'clock in the morning!

The Ship in the Bottle

by Moira Stubley

There were fifteen bedrooms in Wisley Manor. Claudine knew, for she had counted them many times. But Claudine never went into the bedrooms, for she was parlour maid at the rambling old mansion. It was her duty to sweep and dust and polish the four lovely drawing rooms on the ground floor. There was the red parlour, with its rich rosy curtains and velvet cushions. There was the long room, with shining wooden floors. The front parlour was the largest, and looked out over the sweeping lawns of Wisley Manor. But best of all Claudine loved the small parlour, which was really the master's study.

Her master was captain of a ship, and was often away from home, sailing the seven seas. At those times Claudine would spend hours in the small parlour. She knew she would not be disturbed. So she polished every tiny ornament until it shone like sunshine.

She loved every corner of her favourite room. There were pictures of fine romantic ships on every wall. There was a huge tank in which the master kept his collection of underwater plants. Claudine loved to gaze into the water, seeing the pretty coloured plants from all over the world, and dreaming of adventure.

But best of all Claudine loved the ship in the bottle. It was quite a small bottle, made of flawless crystal and it stood on the mantle above the hearth. Somehow, inside the bottle, as if by magic, was a perfect model ship. Its sails looked as if they would love to flutter in the sea breezes. Claudine adored the ship in the bottle, but it made her sad. It was like a prisoner.

So she always gave the crystal bottle an extra special polish. Then, one day, to her horror, Claudine dropped the lovely curved stopper. It tumbled into the hearth and rolled behind the grating.

"No one will notice," she thought. "Certainly not until the master returns. I must ask John the gardener to move the grating and rescue the stopper for me when he has time."

Claudine was always last in the parlours at night, and first to open the curtains each morning. That night, as usual before bed, she filled up each fruit bowl with oranges and pears, peaches and grapes. Then she closed the curtains and left her lovely rooms to sleep until morning.

When Claudine pulled back the curtains in the small parlour next morning she noticed at once! A whole bunch of grapes had been eaten! Whoever had been in the master's parlour overnight? It was quite a mystery.

Claudine was even more puzzled when the same thing happened the next night. She made up her mind to creep down to the small parlour when everyone was asleep. She must find out who was eating the grapes.

So Claudine left the curtains slightly ajar and, just after midnight, she tiptoed down the servants' staircase and crept up to the door of the small parlour. Her heart was thudding as she turned the knob. Whatever would she find inside!

The room was bright with moonlight and in that silver, magic light Claudine saw a wonderful scene. Her beautiful boat had escaped from its bottle. It was sailing gracefully in the master's tank, weaving in and out of the bright tropical plants. And sitting on the table by the fruit bowl was a group of tiny sailors, each no taller than a needle! They were smartly dressed in naval uniforms with pistols and swords at their sides.

Claudine caught her breath in wonder and amazement. Hearing the sound, one of the tiny sailors turned towards her. He bowed low, removing his hat. "Madame," he addressed the startled Claudine, "we have you to thank for our freedom. Since the stopper has been lost from the bottle our ship is able to sail again. I hope you will forgive us for taking some of your delicious grapes!"

Claudine stuttered in amazement. "Oh, there are more grapes in the gardens than cook knows what to do with. I'm pleased you like them." Then, in an eager voice, she begged, "May I watch your ship sailing on the water?"

The sailor led Claudine over to where the lovely ship was sailing in the moonlight. It was such a romantic sight. Claudine could have gazed at it forever.

"You must come down whenever you like, after midnight, of course," the captain of the ship told her.

Claudine clasped her hands in delight. "Thank you, thank you," she cried. "And I shall see that there are always extra grapes in the fruit bowl."

Often after that Claudine shared a magic hour with her lovely ship in her favourite small parlour. But one day, when she was polishing the tables, John the gardener came to her special room.

"I have to clean all the grates," he explained. "So I may as well start here."

Claudine held her breath and, sure enough, she heard the stopper fall from the grating onto the hearth.

"Wherever has this come from?" John asked in surprise. "What a lovely piece of crystal."

Claudine did not reply.

"I'm sure it's been there for years. Do you recognise it, Claudine?"

Still she could not reply.

John went on, "My mother loves glass ornaments. I shall take her this crystal stopper, for I'm sure no one knows where it belongs."

Claudine nodded in agreement and gave a great sigh of relief. Now her beautiful ship would be free for ever and ever, to sail, after midnight, on the moonlit water.

Simon Sparrow

by Moira Stubley

Simon Sparrow should have been his parents' pride and joy. He had a beautiful singing voice, his feathers were thick and glossy, and he had the friendliest disposition. But Simon's parents worried about him all day long and most of the night.

Ever since he had first learnt to fly they had realised that something was wrong. He would flit round the garden from one shrub to another. He would fly up to sit on the birdhouse. But higher than that he would not go! Simon was afraid of heights!

"How can the child protect himself?" Mother Sparrow would ask in dismay. "He's perfectly happy here, among the flowers in the garden, when he should be soaring up through the sky. Imagine it . . . a bird afraid of heights!"

But Simon DID love the flowers. They were his closest friends. All the other birds would fly off to the church steeple or the telegraph poles, while Simon swayed to and fro on a lupin, watching their flight.

"The cats will catch you," Father Sparrow warned him, day after day. But nothing could persuade Simon to fly higher than the birdhouse.

At night, when the other birds returned with tales of their adventures, Simon would show them the lovely pink roses that were beginning to bloom. The colours of the flowers fascinated him. He loved their reds and blues and yellows. He told himself he was quite happy to live in such a colourful garden. But every now and then he would look wistfully up at the blue sky and the white, fluffy clouds.

55

So time went by, and Simon came to know every flower by name. He would sing with delight when a pale purple crocus popped its head out of the ground. He studied the shades and tints of everything that grew in the garden. The colours were his greatest joy, and they helped him forget about flying no higher than the birdhouse.

One bright day Simon was surprised by a sudden heavy shower. Sheltering under a crimson rhododendron he watched the raindrops splattering down. But well before the shower had ended the sun began to shine again. Strong, warm rays of sunshine lit up the sky.

As he gazed upwards, Simon's little beak fell open in amazement! The sky was full of strange and beautiful colours. There was an arc forming, blue like his beloved irises, yellow like the lovely daffodils, purple like the crocus. Why, there was a huge bouquet growing up there in the sky!

Simon could not see properly for the rhododendron leaves, so he flew a little higher, higher, and still higher, until he had a perfect view of the loveliest rainbow you could imagine.

When he looked down, Simon saw to his surprise that the birdhouse looked like a tiny dot far below in the garden. When he looked up he saw nothing at all to be afraid of. From now on Simon's parents WOULD be proud of him. He could fly through the sky like all the other birds. And when it was time to land again what tales he would have to tell the flowers!

The King's Holiday

by R F A Horsfield

The King had just returned from his holidays and was feeling very fed up. "It's not fair," he complained. "Holidays should be much, much longer. Who wants to work, anyway?" Then, suddenly, an idea occurred to him. "Well, my goodness!" he exclaimed. "I *am* the King, after all. If I want a longer holiday, then I shall have one." So he called the Lord Chamberlain and told him that, in future, the King's holiday would begin on the first day of January and end on the last day of December.

"But, Majesty, that means you'll be on holiday all the time!" cried the Chamberlain.

"Yes, that's right," said the King. "But don't worry. I'm going to do the same for you. I want you to issue a decree telling everybody that they will be on holiday for ever. Starting today."

"But, Majesty . . ." began the Lord Chamberlain.

The King waved his hand. "No arguments. Just get on with it," he said, and walked out of the room.

The people were delighted. They surrounded the palace and cheered and shouted and told the King what a fine fellow he was. Then off they went on holiday.

Now the King's brother, Nero, who lived in a nearby castle, had long wanted the throne for himself. So, when he heard the news about everybody being on holiday, he was delighted. He chuckled with glee and called his army to prepare for war.

The very next day the soldiers marched on the palace. When they arrived there was no one to resist them. They found only the King's General, who was reading a book. He looked up in surprise as they entered the room. "What are *you* doing here?" he asked. "I thought everybody was on holiday."

"We are Nero's soldiers," their leader explained. "We have come to seize the palace."

"Oh, is *that* all!" exclaimed the General. "Well, now you've done that, you might as well go off on holiday too."

The soldiers were puzzled. "On holiday? Nobody told *us* anything about a holiday."

So the General explained about the new law and the soldiers grew very excited. "And do we get paid as well?" asked one of them.

"Oh, yes," the General replied. "Come along with me and I'll give you all a year's pay, right now." So they all trooped off to the Treasury and the General gave them the money. "Come back in a year's time and you'll get paid again," he told them. The soldiers thanked him, threw their weapons away, and went off to enjoy their holiday.

When Nero heard about this he was very angry indeed. He hadn't got any more soldiers so he summoned the leader of a band of robbers to meet him. "If you and your men will capture the palace, you may steal anything you wish," he told the robber. "All I want is the throne."

The robber leader thought this a fine idea. He quickly called his men together and, without delay, they made their way to the palace. They rushed in, waving their guns and swords, but there was only the King's General to meet them. He looked up over his glasses.

"Don't tell me *you're* Nero's soldiers, too!" he exclaimed. "I thought you'd all gone on holiday."

The robber leader explained. "We've come to rob the palace," he said. "Nero has told us we can take what we like."

The General sat back in his chair. "Oh, that," he said with a smile. "Yes, you go ahead and take whatever you fancy. I don't know where you're going to sell it, though. Everybody is on holiday."

"On holiday?" echoed the robber chief.

"Nobody told *us* anything about a holiday."

"Well, I don't suppose it matters to *you* chaps," said the General. "You don't work for a living in any case, do you?"

The robbers didn't reply. They just went away and stole as many jewels and precious things as they could carry. Then they took them to the town and tried to sell them. But nobody was interested. Everybody was on holiday and, even though the robbers offered their wares cheaply, they couldn't sell a thing.

They soon became fed up. "There's no point in robbing the palace if we can't sell the things we have stolen," they told their leader. "Perhaps if we take them back the King's General will buy them." After some argument, the leader agreed. Back to the palace they went.

The King's General listened politely as they unfolded their tale of woe. "Well, I'd like to help you," he said, "but I can't really buy back something you have stolen, can I? I'll tell you what I will do, though. I'll give you all a year's pay and send you off on holiday. How about that?"

The robbers were delighted and they, too, took their money and went away to spend it.

The news soon reached Nero and he flew into a fearful rage. He had no more soldiers and he had no more robbers. What was he to do? He thought and thought and, at last, he said: "There's only one thing for it. I'll

seek out the Magron and see if he will help me."

The Magron was a fearsome beast, half man, half dragon, who lived in the depths of the forest. He spent nearly all his life hunting so that he could satisfy his huge appetite. Now he sat, licking his lips, his tummy rumbling, as Nero spoke to him.

"If you seize the palace for me," said Nero, "I will grant you any wish you please. All *I* want is the throne."

The Magron thought for a moment. "I'm getting tired of hunting," he said at last. "If you will give me all the food I can eat and a warm bed at the palace, I will help you."

Nero agreed right away and off went the Magron to capture the palace. On his way he met the King who was fishing in a nearby river. When the King learned what was happening he was greatly alarmed. All his soldiers were on holiday. In fact, *everybody* was on holiday. However could he save his throne?

"Listen," he said to the Magron. "If you will spare my palace, I will give you all the food you want and a warm bed for the rest of your life."

The Magron shook his head. "I have already been promised that," he said.

"Oh, dear," said the King. "Well, perhaps there's something else you wish for?"

The Magron thought. "Well, now you mention it," he said, "I *would* like a nice palace. One like yours, perhaps."

"But that would take years to build," the King protested. "And all my people are on holiday!"

The Magron breathed fire over a clump of trees and watched then crumble to ashes. Then he looked at the King's white face and smiled a terrible smile. "Perhaps you could persuade them to come back," he murmured.

The King groaned and sighed a very deep sigh. The long holiday was over.

The Smallest Seahorse

by Jill Weekes

Selina didn't like being the smallest seahorse. Her brother Simon and her sister Samantha often laughed at her.

Selina was so slow, eating tiny mouthfuls at dinner time, that her food often floated away; Mrs Seahorse had to fetch it. When the family rested in the seaweed patch, their strong tails tightly gripping the long, green, floating strands, Selina's tail couldn't hold on; she had to sleep in Daddy's pouch. Simon and Samantha called her Silly Seahorse!

"It's not fair!" wailed Selina to her mummy. "I can't help it if I'm small! When will I be big like the others?"

"You'll grow up soon enough," Mummy told her, firmly. "Small is sometimes best."

Selina didn't believe her. She longed to be big and strong.

"Do you think I could grow claws like you?" she asked Christopher Crab.

Christopher Crab laughed so much he nearly cracked his shell. "That would look really silly!" he told her. "You're fine just as you are."

"I wish I had long feelers like you!" Selina sighed to Larry Lobster. "They'd make me look much bigger."

Larry chuckled and choked until he gave himself hiccups. "A seahorse with feelers!" he spluttered. "That *would* be a silly creature! I like you much better without them."

Selina groaned in despair. She was sure she would never grow.

Next day, there was great excitement in the seahorse family. "We're going to visit relatives," Mrs Seahorse announced. "It's Uncle Silas's birthday. There'll be a very special tea!"

"Ooh, good!" cheered the seahorse children, who couldn't wait to start.

"It's quite a long swim," warned Daddy. "Selina, do you want to ride on my back?"

"No, thank you," replied Selina. "I can swim by myself!"

The seahorses set off in a line, with Daddy leading the way. They flicked their strong back fins and glided through the water. Selina was last, as usual, but she didn't get left behind. Just as she was feeling tired and longing for a rest, Daddy glanced round at the family, and swam straight into a net!

The others followed him in, before they realized what had happened!

"Help!" moaned Simon and Samantha, as they struggled against the mesh.

"Stop that!" ordered Daddy. "Keep still, while I think what to do."

But Selina knew immediately. She swished her little tail and shot out through a hole in the net. Because she was so small, she could squeeze through quite easily. "I'll go and get help!" she cried. "I won't be long – stay there!"

The big seahorses watched her go, wondering what she could do. It might not be very long before the net was pulled out of the water.

Selina swam as she had never swum before. "I *must* go faster!" she puffed. Soon she arrived at the rock belonging to Christopher Crab.

"Oh, please, come quickly!" she begged, telling him what had happened. Christopher scuttled after her, and they fetched his friend Larry Lobster. Then Selina led them back to the net.

"Dear, dear," muttered Larry Lobster. "We'll soon have you out of there!" He and Christopher used their sharp claws to cut a large hole in the net.

At last, the seahorses were free and swam out just in time. Suddenly, the net started to rise, and disappeared from the water!

"We can't thank you enough," said Mrs Seahorse to Christopher and Larry.

"We were very glad to help," Christopher replied. "But without Selina we couldn't have rescued you."

Simon and Samantha were especially nice to Selina. "I'll never call you silly again," promised Simon. "You were very brave."

"I wish I was small like you," sighed Samantha.

"Oh no, we can't change what we are," replied her little sister. "But I'm glad small is sometimes best!"